COUPON MADNESS

Adapted by Annie Auerbach

SCHOLASTIC INC.
New York Toronto London Auckland Sydney
Mexico City New Delhi Hong Kong Buenos Aires

ISBN-13: 978-0-545-10040-3
ISBN-10: 0-545-10040-2

Published by Scholastic Inc.

12 11 10 9 8 7 6 5 4 3 2 1 9 10 11 12/0

Designed by Angela Jun
Printed in the U.S.A.
First printing, January 2009

Hi! I'm WordGirl.

Captain Huggy Face and I are from the planet Lexicon.

We crash-landed on Earth when I was a baby.

Everyone here knows us as Becky Botsford and Bob.

But secretly, I use my superstrength and word power to fight evil villains.

Worrrd up!

One afternoon, Becky and her family were doing some shopping. They were at the only grocery store in town that still allowed monkeys—so Bob could come along. Her brother, T.J., stared at a life-size cutout of WordGirl.

"Can you imagine if she came to life right now?" T.J. said dreamily. "What do you think she'd say?"

"That you have crumbs on your face?" replied Becky with a smile.

T.J. didn't laugh, so Becky and Bob went in search of free samples.

30% more snappy!
SNAPPY SNAPS
30% more snappy!
SNAPPY SNAPS
30% more snappy!
SNAPPY SNAPS
30% more snappy!
SNAPPY SNAPS
30% more snappy!
SNAPPY SNAPS

Meanwhile, on the other side of town, Granny May was doing some shopping of her own at the bank. She handed the teller a coupon that was good for "One Free Toaster . . . and ALL the Money in the Bank!" As she left with her loot, a guard stopped her. But Granny May showed him the coupon, too.

"Wow! That's a bargain!" he said.

Granny May's next stop was the used car lot. She flashed a coupon to the owner of the lot and drove off in a big truck loaded with all the cars. She didn't have to pay for any of them!

Then Granny May headed to the grocery store. She walked up to the store manager. "This coupon entitles me to 2-for-1 on cans of tuna," she said. "And the combination to your safe!"

"Really?" asked the manager. "I don't remember printing that."

With an evil look in her eyes, Granny May pulled out her knitting needles. *WHOOSH!* Purple yarn shot out of the needles and wrapped around the manager until he couldn't move.

"Ha, ha, ha!" laughed Granny May.

"Now then, what's the combination to the safe?" Granny May asked sweetly.

"Mmmp-mmph," grumbled the manager. His mouth was covered in yarn.

Just then Becky turned the corner and saw Granny May. *Hmm . . . looks like trouble,* she thought. She ducked behind a Snappy Snap cookie display, and in a flash, Becky changed into her WordGirl outfit. "Worrrd up!" she shouted.

"Let the store manager go, Granny!" WordGirl demanded.

BLAM! Granny May shot her web of yarn at the pair. But they dodged the fast-moving string. It landed on a shelf between them.

"Ha, ha! You missed!" said WordGirl.

Granny had an evil look in her eye. "Oh, I did, huh? You kids think you know everything."

Then Granny May yanked her knitting needles, causing the yarn to pull down boxes of food from the shelves. The food fell all around WordGirl and Captain Huggy Face. They were trapped!

With a push of a button on her pearl necklace, Granny May's armor appeared. "Now, excuse me. I have to go finish my shopping." She rose into the air and zoomed off!

WordGirl and Huggy Face caught up with Granny May at a local jewelry store. She was trying to use another fake coupon. This one was for "One Free Jewelry Store and Everything In It."

"You again?!" Granny exclaimed. She shook her head. "I don't understand why a pretty superhero like you would let a rat follow her around."

"Huggy is a monkey, not a rat," said WordGirl. But Granny May wasn't listening.

Granny May sprayed some awful-smelling perfume into the air. It formed a stinky green cloud, which was the perfect cover for her to grab all the jewels in the store!

But as Granny May suited up in her armor and flew off, Huggy took a flying leap and grabbed onto her foot. He held on tight as she flew up into the sky.

Back at her lair, Granny was planning her biggest caper yet: a coupon that gave her control of the whole city! (Plus one free hair appointment. She *had* to look good if she was going to control the city!)

Just then, Captain Huggy Face jumped down, striking a dramatic "Huggy Fu" pose. He was ready for action!

Granny reached into her hair and pulled out her knitting needles. All of a sudden . . . *WHAM!* Huggy's hands and feet were tied up in unbreakable yarn.

Just in time, WordGirl appeared. "Your coupon-cutting days are over, Granny May!" she declared.

Granny May began to sob. "Oh, I guess you've caught me. It's just so hard for a little old lady in this big old world. Everything is so expensive! Is it so wrong to hunt for bargains?"

"You're not bargain hunting!" replied WordGirl. "A *bargain* is when you buy something for a lot less than it's worth. What you did is called *stealing*. You made those coupons yourself in order to get free stuff."

"Well, free is the best bargain there is!" Granny replied.

"We'll see how good you really are at bargain hunting when I destroy your coupon-making machine!" said WordGirl. She charged toward it.

Granny quickly reached into her purse and grabbed a handful of old mints. "Let's see how you fare against these Petrified Purse Mints!" She whipped them up into a mini-tornado.

"*Aaagh!*" cried WordGirl. "They're so . . . minty! They're burning my eyes!"

WordGirl felt around a nearby table and located a pair of oversized sunglasses. "That's better!" she said with relief. Then she grabbed an umbrella and opened it up. The mints bounced off of it and onto the printing press with ferocious minty power.

"No! My precious coupons!" cried Granny.

WordGirl and Captain Huggy Face rolled Granny May up in the carpet, and tied her up with a bow.

When the police arrived, they took her away.

"I'll get you, WordGirl!" vowed Granny May.

With Granny May behind bars, the citizens of the city could safely hunt for honest bargains once again, thanks to WordGirl and Captain Huggy Face.

Wordoko

Hello! I'm Beau Handsome and here are today's puzzles. Good luck!

Let's begin with a Wordoko puzzle. Fill in the grid below so that every row, column, and box contains the letters named under the board. The diagonal will spell out a word! To give you a clue, the words are things Granny May used in the story.

y			a
n		y	r
r		a	n

letters: nayr

	n	t	
	i	m	n
i			
		i	t

letters: itmn

Crossword Puzzle

Great job! Are you ready for another puzzle? Read the clues below and write the correct word in the squares.

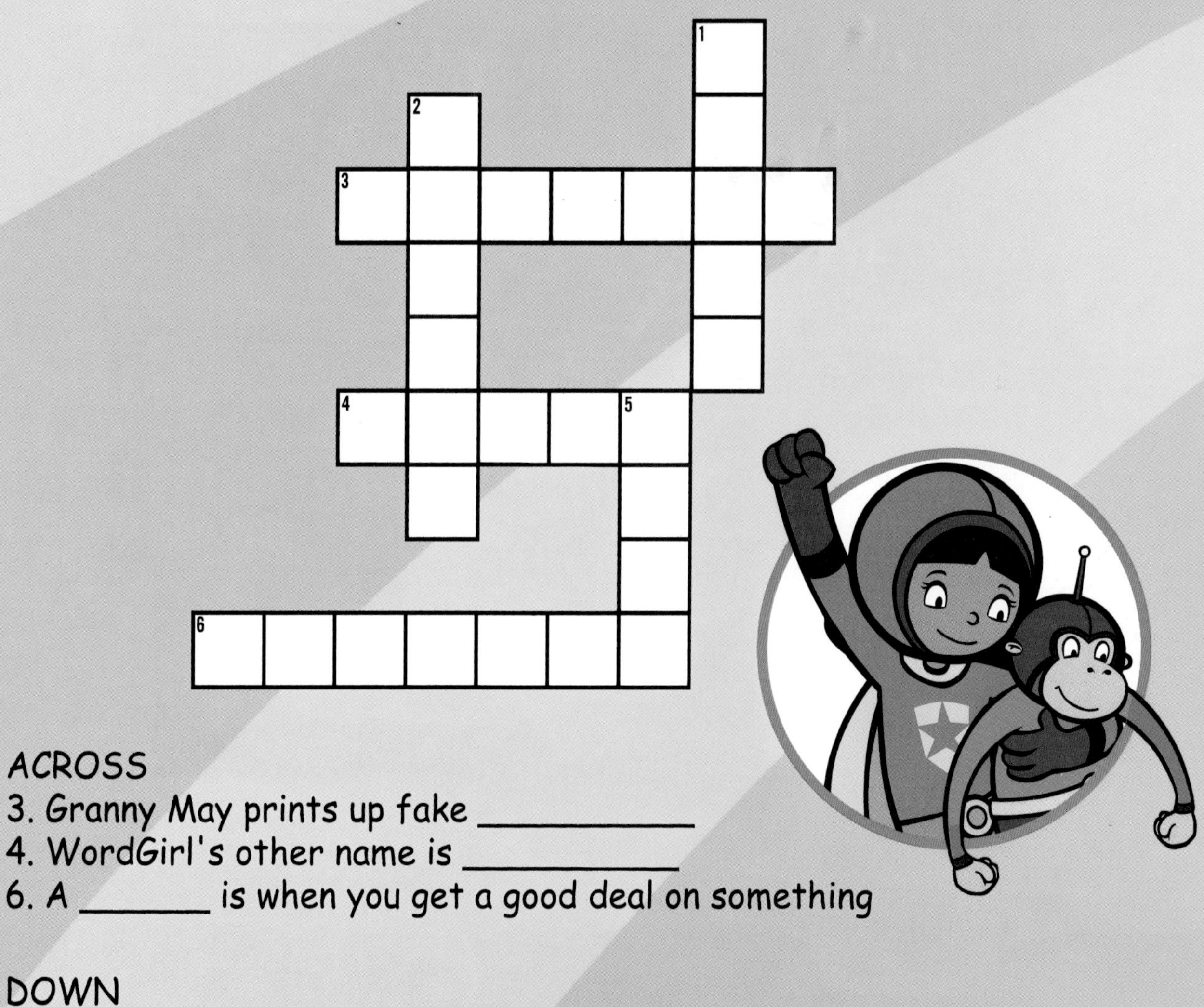

ACROSS
3. Granny May prints up fake ___________
4. WordGirl's other name is ___________
6. A ______ is when you get a good deal on something

DOWN
1. Petrified Purse _____
2. Captain Huggy Face is this type of animal
5. Granny May used this to attack the grocery store manager

Answer Key

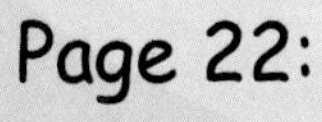

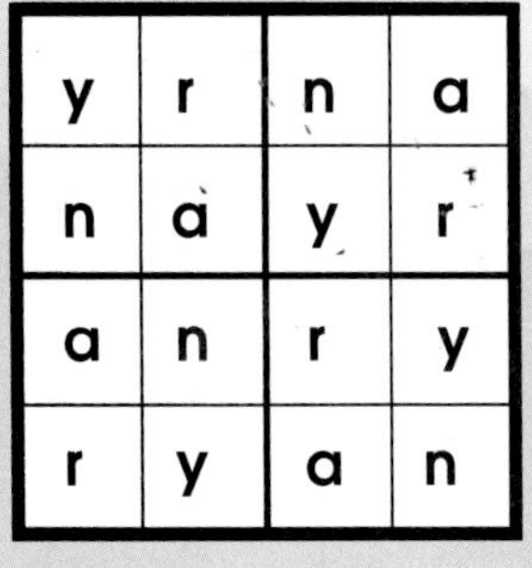

y	r	n	a
n	a	y	r
a	n	r	y
r	y	a	n

yarn

m	n	t	i
t	i	m	n
i	t	n	m
n	m	i	t

mint

Page 23:

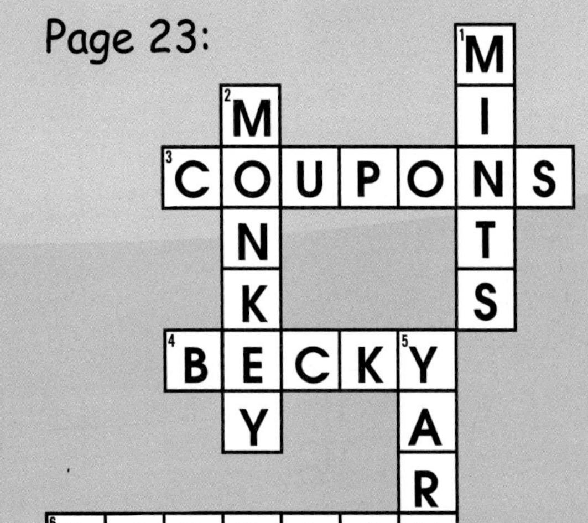

All right. That's it for today's puzzles. See you next time!